The
Greatest Gift

ISBN 979-8-88685-775-7 (paperback)
ISBN 979-8-88685-776-4 (digital)

Christian Faith Publishing
832 Park Avenue
Meadville, PA 16335
www.christianfaithpublishing.com

Printed in the United States of America

The Greatest Gift

Tanya Boynay

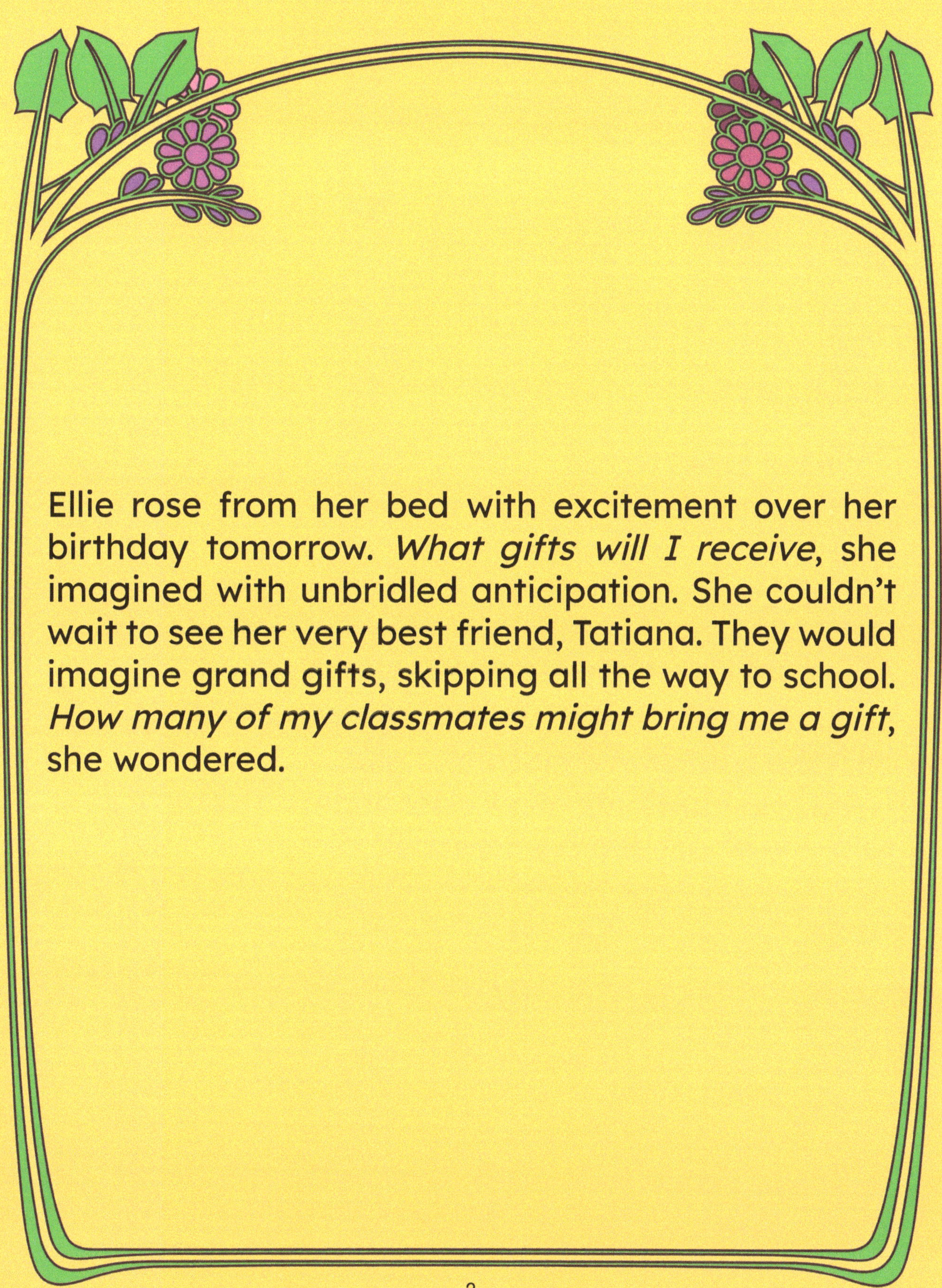

Ellie rose from her bed with excitement over her birthday tomorrow. *What gifts will I receive*, she imagined with unbridled anticipation. She couldn't wait to see her very best friend, Tatiana. They would imagine grand gifts, skipping all the way to school. *How many of my classmates might bring me a gift*, she wondered.

“Ellie! Ellie!”

“Oh, yes, Dad,” Ellie answered smiling up at her dad.

“Where were you?”, he said with a grin.

“Oh, I was just thinking about all the gifts I will receive for my birthday tomorrow. I am turning ten, you know. It’s a special birthday. Double digits and all,” she said with a sideways grin.

“Gifts, huh?” her dad questioned. “Have I ever told you about *the greatest gift?*”

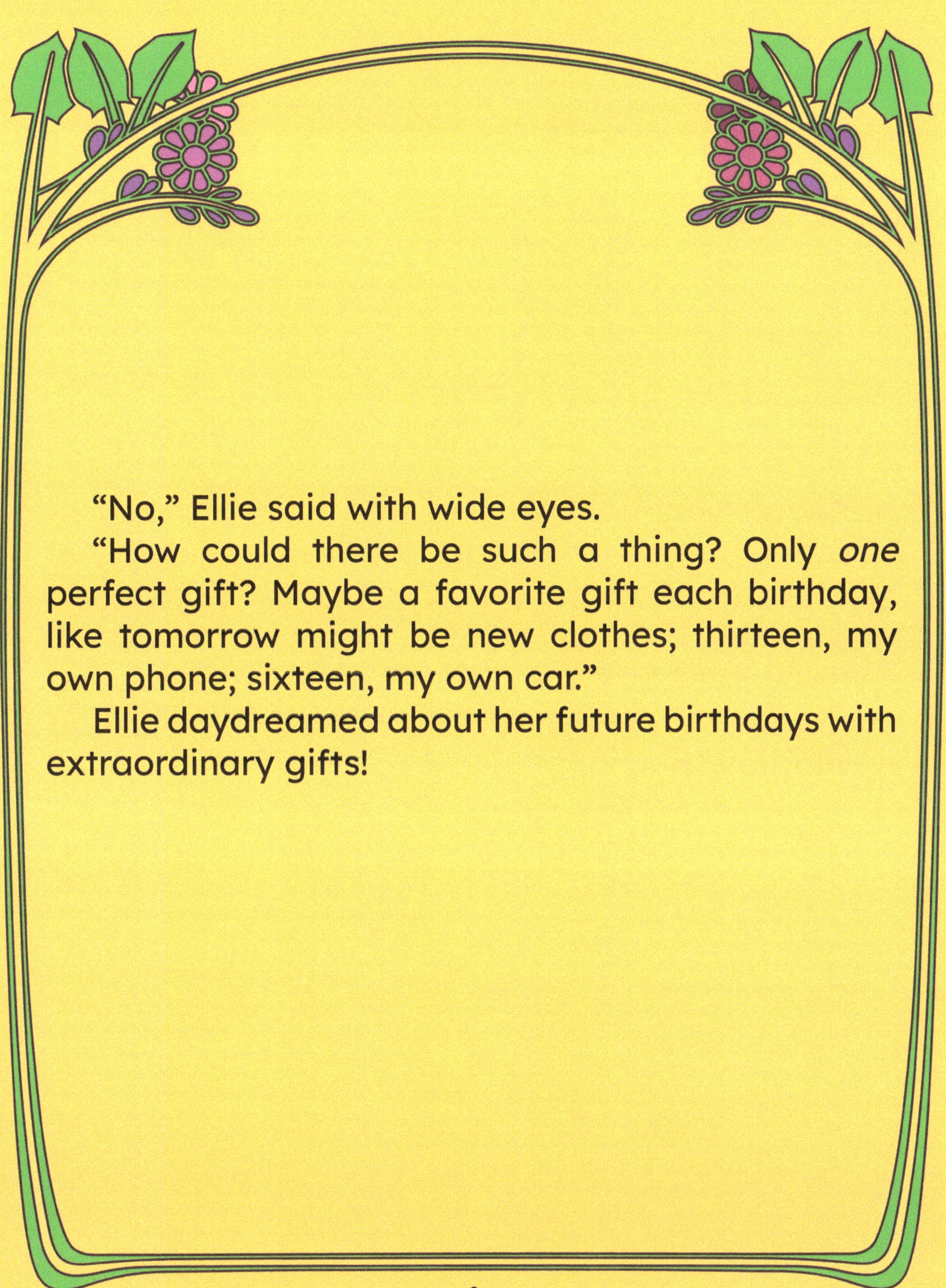

"No," Ellie said with wide eyes.

"How could there be such a thing? Only *one* perfect gift? Maybe a favorite gift each birthday, like tomorrow might be new clothes; thirteen, my own phone; sixteen, my own car."

Ellie daydreamed about her future birthdays with extraordinary gifts!

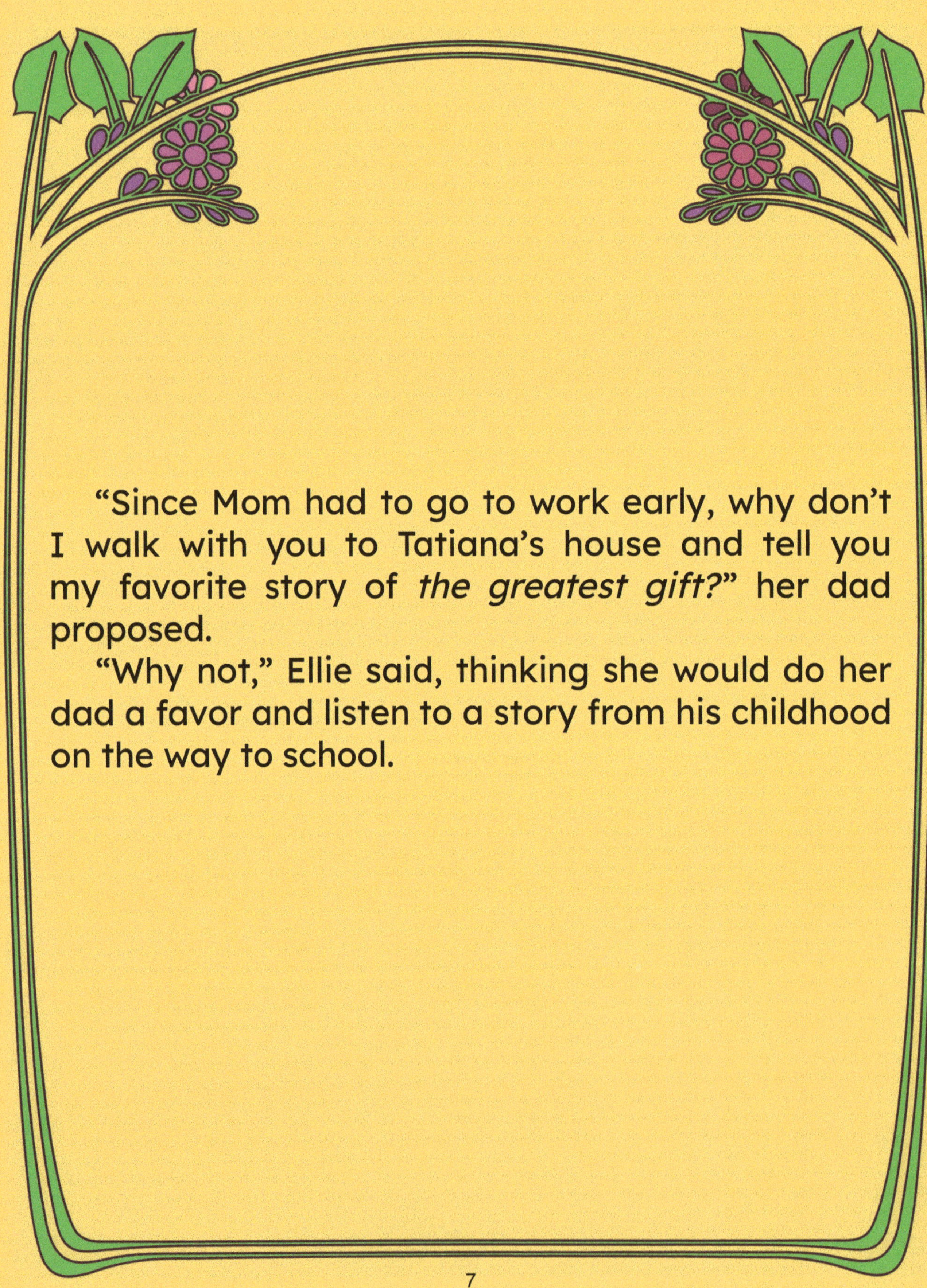

"Since Mom had to go to work early, why don't I walk with you to Tatiana's house and tell you my favorite story of *the greatest gift?*" her dad proposed.

"Why not," Ellie said, thinking she would do her dad a favor and listen to a story from his childhood on the way to school.

Ellie felt so happy the sun was bright and warm today, and the flowers were beginning to bloom. She even caught a glimpse of a rainbow.

Lost in thought, she was startled as her dad began the story that meant so much to him.

"It's really rather simple," he started. "It's just not easy for everyone."

Ellie was confused! How could a gift be simple but not easy? This just didn't make sense. She wondered if her dad had gotten enough sleep last night!

"The greatest gift is salvation that comes through Jesus."

"Salva...what?" Ellie asked.

"Salvation, to be with Jesus always!"

"I have heard you and Mom talk about Jesus, but how is that a gift I can use now?" Ellie questioned.

"Well," her dad answered, "if you and Jesus know you are receiving this gift, then you can count on Jesus to be with you every minute of every day until you join Him in heaven. Think about it as if you have your best friend with you all the time!"

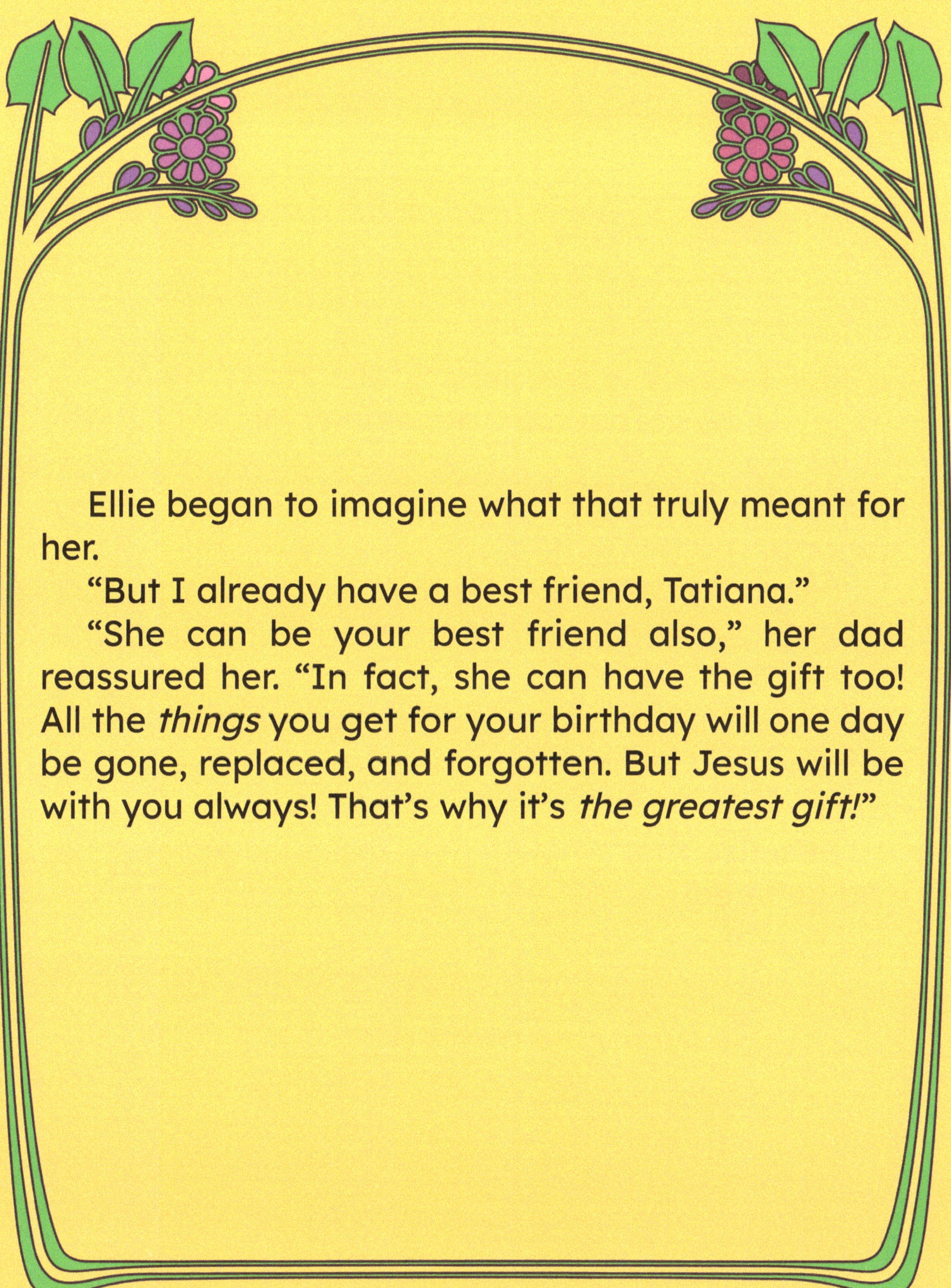

Ellie began to imagine what that truly meant for her.

"But I already have a best friend, Tatiana."

"She can be your best friend also," her dad reassured her. "In fact, she can have the gift too! All the *things* you get for your birthday will one day be gone, replaced, and forgotten. But Jesus will be with you always! That's why it's *the greatest gift!*"

"But how do I get this gift? I don't have any money. Unless of course, I get money for my birthday tomorrow."

Maybe there is a pot of gold at the end of that rainbow, she thought.

"Did you and Mom get me money for my birthday?"

"It's free," Dad explained. "You don't need any money. You just need to love Jesus with all your heart and believe this gift came from him."

"How can something so grand be free?" Ellie asked.

"Because that's how much Jesus loves you." her dad beamed!

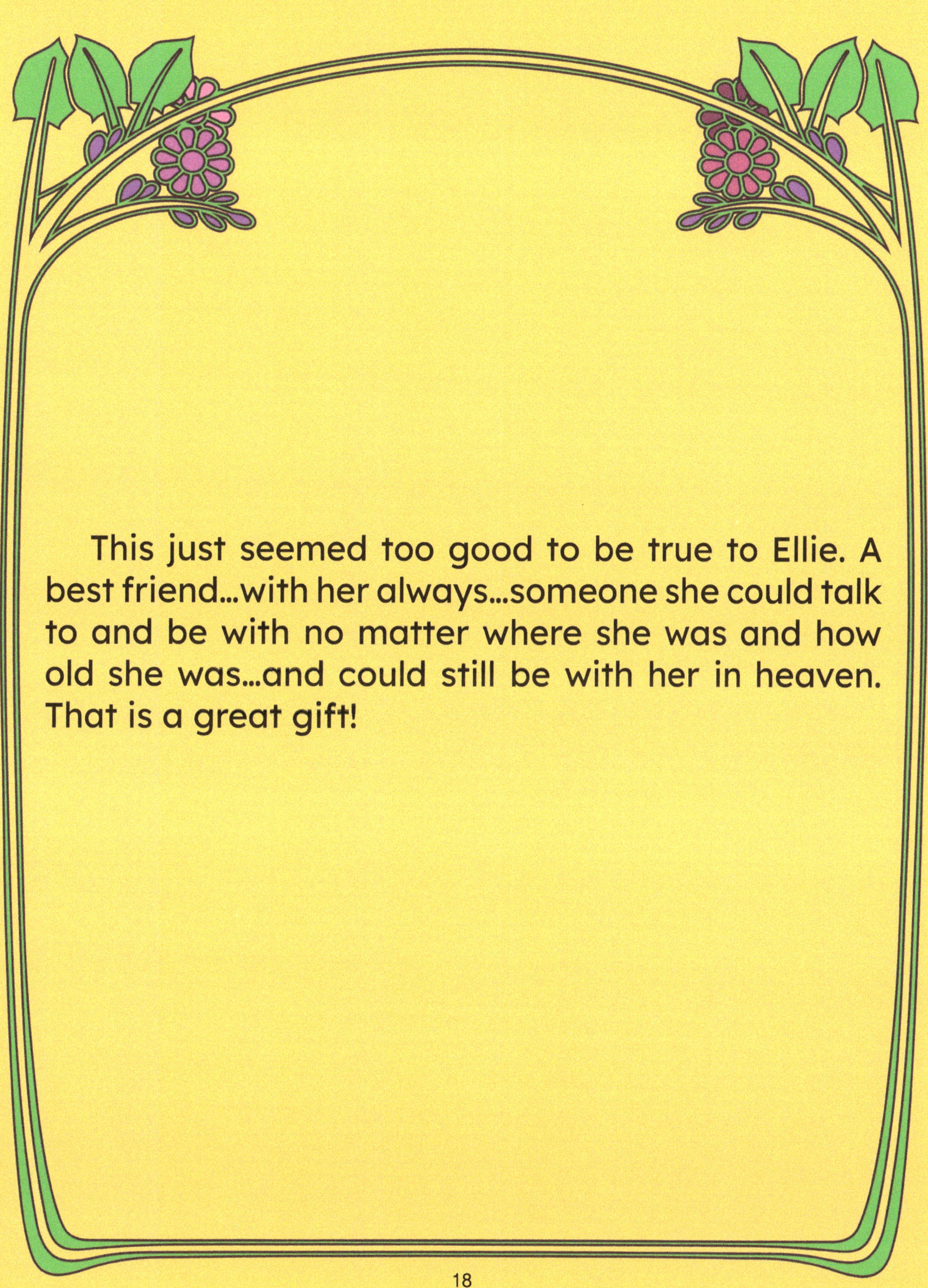

This just seemed too good to be true to Ellie. A best friend...with her always...someone she could talk to and be with no matter where she was and how old she was...and could still be with her in heaven. That is a great gift!

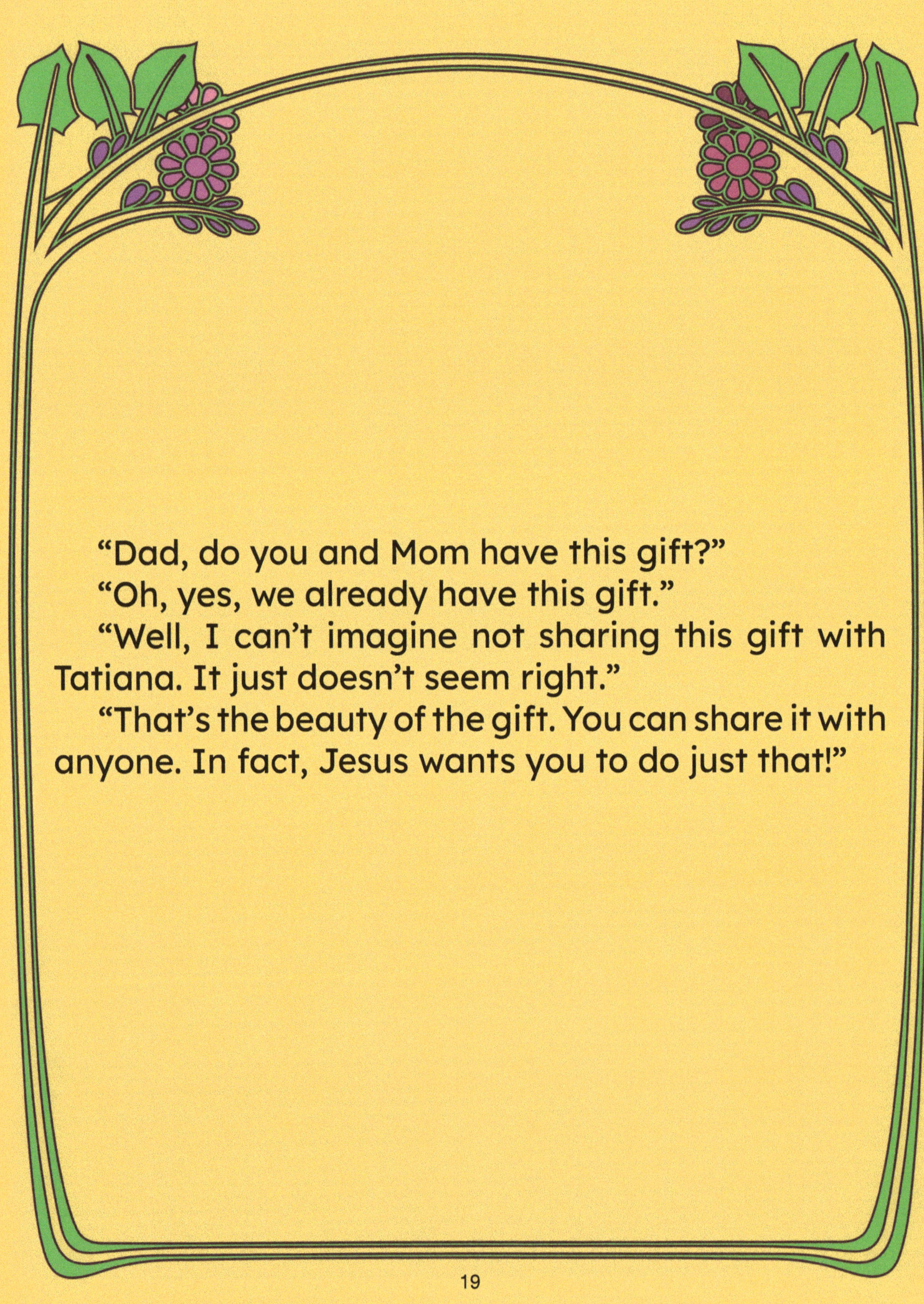

"Dad, do you and Mom have this gift?"

"Oh, yes, we already have this gift."

"Well, I can't imagine not sharing this gift with Tatiana. It just doesn't seem right."

"That's the beauty of the gift. You can share it with anyone. In fact, Jesus wants you to do just that!"

Filled with unexplainable joy, Ellie's thoughts changed from birthday gifts she might receive to her best friend, Tatiana, and sharing this gift with her.

Seeing her friend waving from the porch, Ellie said goodbye to her dad and shouted, "Tatiana, Tatiana, do I have a story for you!"

The End

About the Author

Tanya currently lives in the majestic Pacific Northwest. Being a Christian for most of her adult life, Tanya loves the Lord with all her capacity. The decision to leave public school teaching and follow an author's path has led to the creation of this book, guided and nurtured by the Holy Spirit. Her husband of thirty-five years and two children are her greatest adventure and accomplishment. When not tending to everyday needs, the outdoor is forever calling her to play and frolic amongst the earthly natural beauty God has blessed us with since creation.